I think about your positive, carefree outlook. Always keep it.

I remember that this is your most favorite season of the year.

I think about your unstoppable sense of curiosity.

I contemplate the person you're becoming and wonder what exciting opportunities you'll have in your lifetime.

I think about the wisdom you have shared with me through the years.

I hear your favorite song on the radio.

I only have to look at you and by your expression I know what you're thinking.

I think to myself how you have enriched my life.

you are creative and use your imagination.

you pick me a bouquet of tiny wildflowers.

we walk barefoot in the sand.

I wake in the morning and remember you were with me throughout the night in my dreams.

I hear the sound of your voice.

Love with your whole heart ♥

Linda Kranz

Love you When...

by
Linda Kranz

Photography by Klaus Kranz

TAYLOR TRADE PUBLISHING
Lanham • New York • Boulder
Toronto • Plymouth, UK

Published by TAYLOR TRADE PUBLISHING

An imprint of The Rowman & Littlefield Publishing Group, Inc.
4501 Forbes Boulevard, Suite 200, Lanham, Maryland 20706
www.rowman.com

10 Thornbury Road, Plymouth PL6 7PP, United Kingdom

Distributed by National Book Network

British Library Cataloguing in Publication Information Available

Library of Congress Cataloging-in-Publication Data Available
ISBN 978-1-58979-703-1 (cloth)
ISBN 978-1-58979-704-8 (electronic)

Printed in Huizhou, Guangdong, PRC, China December 2014

For Jessica and Nik

We love you up to the moon.

—M&D

"Do you think of me during the day?" you ask.
"Yes," I say as I close my eyes for a moment and smile.

In a voice as soft as a whisper you say,
"Tell me when."

"I love you and think of you
all day, every day, always," I say.

I love you when . . .

the first rays of sun

light up the early morning sky.

I love you when the **sweet scent of flowers** drifts through **an open window in the spring.**

I love you when a gentle breeze rustles through our backyard wind chime, and a peaceful sound fills the air.

I love
you when
cheerful
little birds
arrive to sing
us their own
distinctive
songs.

I love you when a brilliant

rainbow

peeks out through the clouds
after a drenching rainstorm
has cooled off
a sizzling summer day.

I love you when we're out on a walk,

and we find

a new rock

to add to our amazing collection.

I love you when we notice

fluffy white clouds

in the deep blue sky,
and we search for familiar shapes
as they float by.

I love you when shooting stars appear bright and steady,

and we watch them sparkle

as

they

fall

to decorate the night.

I love you when

colorful

leaves

tumble

in the crisp fall air
and land softly
on the ground.

I love you when

snow covers the winter landscape,

and everything is so incredibly

s t i l l .

I love you when
the house is quiet late at night,
and thoughts of you

make me smile.

I love you when I turn the page on the Calendar,

and I wonder what remarkable discoveries we will share in the months to come.

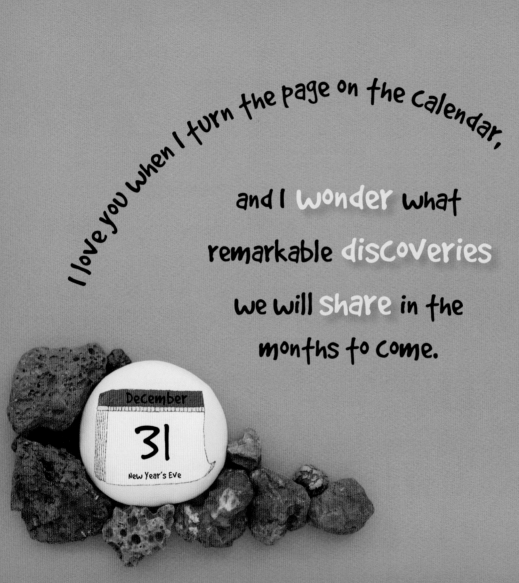

December

31

New Year's Eve

"No matter where I am or what I am doing,
I will always love you," I say.

"I love you, too," you say,
as you wrap your arms around me.

I take your hands in mine.
" Day and night. Night and day.
I love you through all seasons."

Love You When...

you listen so intently when I speak.

we watch fireflies blink and glow on a warm summer night.

I remember all the times your thoughtfulness has brightened my day.

we are the only ones out on a walk as the first snow of the season begins to fall.

a ladybug flies close, so you offer your hand for her to rest awhile.

I realize that you've always encouraged me to be the best I can be.

you're enthusiastic about learning something new.

I notice things you do that show me just how much you love me.

we spend time together and your vibrant energy rubs off on me.

I pull your favorite book off the shelf, and we take turns reading the story together.